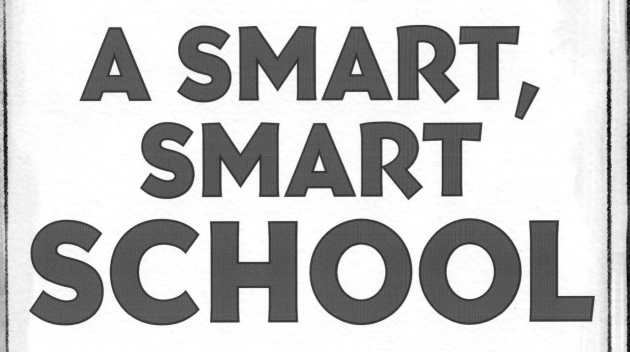

A SMART, SMART SCHOOL

By Sharon Creech

Pictures by
Anait Semirdzhyan

HARPER
An Imprint of HarperCollinsPublishers

A Smart, Smart School

Text copyright © 2023 by Sharon Creech

Illustrations copyright © 2023 by Anait Semirdzhyan

All rights reserved. Manufactured in the United States.

No part of this book may be used or reproduced in any manner whatsoever without written permission except
in the case of brief quotations embodied in critical articles and reviews. For information address HarperCollins
Children's Books, a division of HarperCollins Publishers, 195 Broadway, New York, NY 10007.

www.harpercollinschildrens.com

Library of Congress Control Number: 2022935787

ISBN 978-0-06-305961-0

The artist used Procreate to create the digital illustrations for this book.

23 24 25 26 27   PC   10 9 8 7 6 5 4 3 2 1

❖

First Edition

For smart, smart schools everywhere, including
three in which I've worked:
*
TASIS The American School in England
The American School in Switzerland
The Pennington School (NJ)
*
and for Lyle, with luverino
—S.C.

For Lev—my smart, smart husband and friend
—A.S.

At the beginning and end of each day, the principal, Mr. Keene, rang the school bell. Tillie, who was the first student to arrive and the last to leave, often helped him.

Mr. Keene loved his fine, fine school. He loved to stroll up and down the halls looking at the fine, fine students and the fine, fine teachers. He loved to watch the students drawing and painting and reading and singing.

He felt so proud to be their principal that some days he thought his buttons would burst.

But one day, something else burst. His appendix! Poor Mr. Keene. Away to the hospital he went.

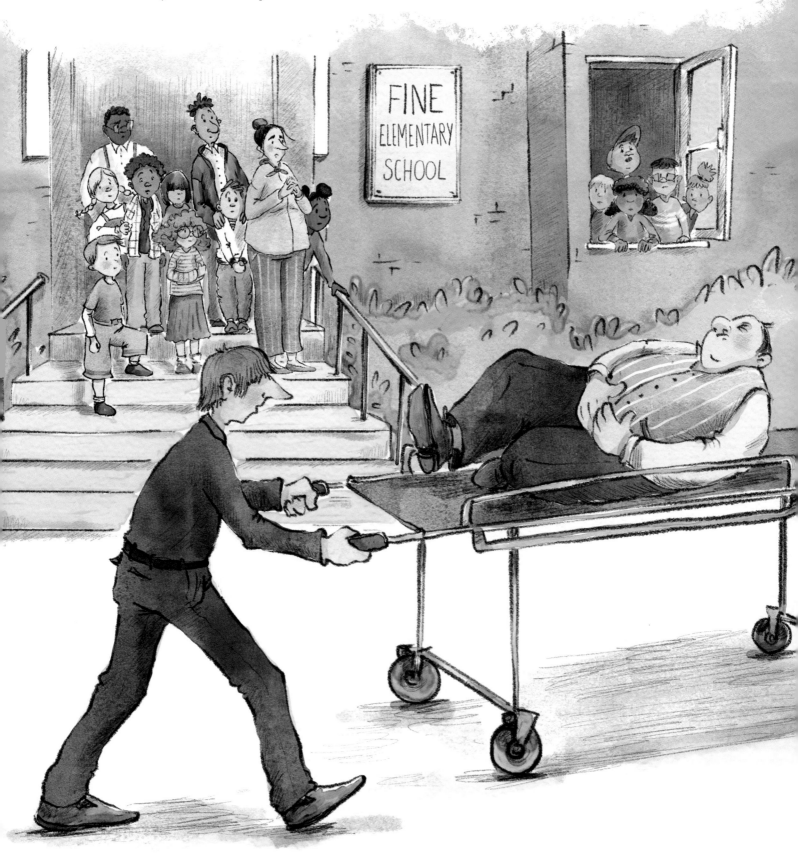

Tillie was worried. Would Mr. Keene get better?

A new principal arrived. His name was Mr. Tatters, and he was a serious man. He did not smile. He did not laugh. He marched up and down the halls, glaring at the students and the teachers.

He stomped into one room where Tillie was sitting nearest the door. "What's that you're doing?" Mr. Tatters demanded.

"We're making get-well cards," Tillie said. "For Mr. Keene."

"Come with me," Mr. Tatters said. He led Tillie to another room. "And what is going on there?" he asked.

"They're making a banner for Mr. Keene," Tillie said. "A get-well banner."

Mr. Tatters marched up and down the halls with Tillie at his side. They saw children making cards and banners and posters and paper flowers. In the last room, children were scribbling on the board.

"There!" he said. "What is going on there?"

Tillie said, "They're writing a song for Mr. Keene. A get-well song. It's nearly done. Would you like to hear it?"

"No, I would not," Mr. Tatters said.

The next day, as all the children were in their classrooms working on their cards and banners and posters and flowers and songs, Mr. Tatters made an announcement.

"This is a school," he said, "and in order to be a smart, smart school, we should be taking tests."

"Uh-oh," Tillie thought.

"We will have lots and lots of tests," Mr. Tatters said.

The students and the teachers were worried.

"And we will not be making any more cards and banners and posters and flowers and songs. When we return on Monday, we will be taking important tests. This will be a smart, smart school."

And so, on Monday, the students took tests all day long.

And on Tuesday, they took tests all day long.

At home, Tillie's dog, Beans, pulled at her shoelaces.
Her little brother tugged at her sleeve.

"Aren't you going to play with us?" he said.

"I can't," Tillie said. "I have to study for these tests.
I have a million tests!"

On Wednesday and Thursday, Tillie and her friends took tests all day long. One of Tillie's teachers said, "I can't think of any more questions to ask!"

Another said, "I can't grade another test!"

Tillie said, "I have no more answers."

At home, Beans lay at Tillie's feet. "My brain is empty, empty, empty!" Tillie said.

Her little brother handed her an orange. "For your brain," he said.

On Friday, Tillie and her friends took tests all day long, and at the end of the day, the students and the teachers limped home.

But on Saturday, they all went to the hospital. Inside, Tillie spoke with a nurse.

"I see," said the nurse. "Tell them to stand over there, on the grass."

When the students and teachers saw the nurse and Mr. Keene at a window, they held up their cards and banners and posters and flowers and they sang their song.

"Mr. Keene, Mr. Keene,
please get well!
Please come back and
ring the bell.

"Mr. Keene, Mr. Keene,
please get well!
We miss you tons
'cause you're so swell!"

They sang their song loudly and proudly. They waved their cards
and banners and posters and flowers.
Mr. Keene left the window.

Five minutes passed.

Ten minutes.

The students and the teachers felt sad, sad, sad. "I guess we'd better go home now," Tillie said.

But then the door of the hospital opened, and out came the nurse pushing a wheelchair, and in the wheelchair was Mr. Keene in his white hospital gown with a yellow blanket over his knees.

Tillie wheeled him around so that he could examine the cards and banners and posters and flowers. Mr. Keene smiled and smiled.

On Monday, Mr. Keene returned to his school. He helped Mr. Tatters pack up his papers. "Bye-bye," he said. And after Mr. Tatters left, Mr. Keene made an announcement.

"I have been studying all the tests you have taken, and I am extremely concerned."

"Uh-oh," Tillie thought.

"These tests definitely show that something is missing."

The students and the teachers were worried.

Tillie went to Mr. Keene's office. "Mr. Keene," she said. "Our brains are empty."

"Empty? But that beautiful song—those posters and flowers? Didn't those come from your brains?"

"That was before the tests," Tillie said.

"Aha," Mr. Keene said. "I see."

That afternoon, Mr. Keene made another announcement.
"I have discovered what is missing from your tests," he said.

"Uh-oh," Tillie thought.

"There are no drawings, no beautiful colors, no little
poems. These tests do not *sing* to me!" Mr. Keene said. "And
so tomorrow—and all week—we will have one more big test!"

Groans filled the room.

"We will have a test to see if we can go one whole week without a test!"
A huge, enormous cheer went up throughout the school.

"And," Mr. Keene added, "we will only be able to draw and sing and dance and write poems this week!"

Another huge, enormous cheer went up throughout the school and sailed out the windows and into the air.

That week, Mr. Keene went around to all the classes and watched the students drawing and painting and writing poems and singing.

He gave each student a button: A SMART, SMART STUDENT.

And he gave each teacher a button: A SMART, SMART TEACHER.

So, of course, the students made a huge, colorful banner, which they hung on Mr. Keene's office door:

All that week, the students painted and drew and sang, and they did not take any tests, not one single one.

"Someday," Mr. Keene said, "we will take a test or two. Someday. But not this day."

If you pass that school, even now, you might see Mr. Keene ringing the bell. And you might also see a beautifully painted banner out front:

A SMART, SMART SCHOOL

And beneath it, another banner:

WITH SMART, SMART STUDENTS, AND SMART, SMART TEACHERS, AND A SMART, SMART PRINCIPAL TOO!